D0206480

the CRitteR club

Marion and the Girls' Getaway

by Callie Barkley 💜 illustrated by Tracy Bishop

LITTLE SIMON

New York London Toronto Sydney New Delhi

If you purchased this book without a cover, you should be aware that this book is stolen property. It was reported as "unsold and destroyed" to the publisher, and neither the author nor the publisher has received any payment for this "stripped book."

This book is a work of fiction. Any references to historical events, real people, or real places are used fictitiously. Other names, characters, places, and events are products of the author's imagination, and any resemblance to actual events or places or persons, living or dead, is entirely coincidental.

LITTLE SIMON

An imprint of Simon & Schuster Children's Publishing Division · 1230 Avenue of the Americas, New York, New York 10020 · First Little Simon paperback edition September 2019 · Copyright © 2019 by Simon & Schuster, Inc. All rights reserved, including the right of reproduction in whole or in part in any form. LITTLE SIMON is a registered trademark of Simon & Schuster, Inc., and associated colophon is a trademark of Simon & Schuster, Inc. For information about special discounts for bulk purchases, please contact Simon & Schuster Special Sales at 1-866-506-1949 or business@simonandschuster.com. The Simon & Schuster Speakers Bureau can bring authors to your live event. For more information or to book an event contact the Simon & Schuster Speakers Bureau at 1-866-248-3049 or visit our website at www.simonspeakers.com. Designed by Laura Roode. The text of this book was set in ITC Stone Informal Std.

Manufactured in the United States of America 0819 MTN

10 9 8 7 6 5 4 3 2 1

Cataloging-in-Publication Data for this title is available from the Library of Congress.

ISBN 978-1-5344-4870-4 (hc)

ISBN 978-1-5344-4869-8 (pbk)

ISBN 978-1-5344-4871-1 (eBook)

Table of Contents

Chapter 1

Perfect Weekend, Perfect Idea

The fire crackled in the fireplace. Marion Ballard snuggled into her cozy blanket. She turned the last page of the book in her lap. It was the latest in one of her favorite series, Hero Horses. And it was ending just the way Marion had hoped. The stallion carried the injured rider five miles through a storm to safety!

Marion closed the book with a *snap* and sighed. This was turning out to be a pretty perfect weekend so far!

The night before, Marion had a sleepover with Amy, Liz, and Ellie. They were her best friends—and her partners at The Critter Club, an animal rescue shelter they had started in their town of Santa Vista.

The girls had a sleepover almost every Friday. This one was at Ellie's house. They had made tacos for dinner—tofu tacos for Liz, who was vegan. They'd watched a movie about a dolphin. Then, this morning, Mr. Mitchell had made waffles for breakfast.

And tonight was such a cozy evening at home! Marion loved it when her mom made a fire in the fireplace. She loved reading by the warmth. She didn't even mind playing Go Fish with her little sister, Gabby, ten times! As long as it was by the fire.

Hmm, thought Marion. What should she do next? She scanned a nearby bookshelf. Should she reread one of the other Hero Horses books?

Marion's eyes fell on some big leather-bound albums. Photo albums! Oh, she could look at those for hours. Some of them went way back. They had photos of her mom and dad when they were Marion's age! Some of the albums had photos of Marion as a baby. And photos of Marion as a toddler. And photos of toddler Marion with baby Gabby.

But Marion pulled down the newest album. She knew it had photos from the past year. Gabby in her school play. Marion holding Teddy, her class's pet hamster.

Marion flipped the page. Here were photos of last year's ski trip. Marion in her ski helmet. The Ballard family at the top of the mountain. A moose they'd spotted near the ski cabin. It was actually their cousin Lou's cabin. But he let the Ballards use it at least once a year.

Suddenly, Marion had an idea. A perfectly fantastic idea. It combined so many of her favorite things: friends, fun, the ski cabin, and wildlife sightings!

But first, she had to get her mom and dad to agree.

Chapter 2

The Secret Plan

Marion found her parents in the kitchen. Her mom was putting away dinner leftovers. Her dad was making tea.

"Dad," Marion said, "have I told you I *love* your mint tea? You're a tea master. The best!"

Mr. Ballard smiled. "I thought you didn't like tea," he said to Marion.

13

"Oh . . . um . . . when *you* make it I do!" Marion stammered.

Mr. Ballard went back to stirring his tea. Marion stood silently, watching him.

Mrs. Ballard came over. She put her arm around Marion. "Is there something *else* we can do for you?"

Marion laughed. They knew she was trying to get on their good side.

She decided to come right out and say it. "Can I invite Liz, Ellie, and Amy up to the ski cabin?" she asked.

Marion's parents looked at each other. Her dad raised his eyebrows. It was his "what do you think?" look.

Her mom smiled and shrugged. It was her "I don't see why not" look.

Before they said a word, Marion started jumping up and down.

"Oh, thank you, thank you!" Marion cheered. She gave them each a hug.

"We were already thinking of taking you and Gabby up there next weekend," Mr. Ballard said. "Lou said yes. So the timing is perfect!"

Mrs. Ballard warned Marion not to get too excited—yet. "It's up to the girls' parents," she said. "We'll call them all and talk it over."

Mrs. Ballard went to the phone. As she looked up the Purvis's number, Marion gasped.

"Mom! Could you ask the parents to keep it a secret? To not tell my friends?"

Marion was set to host the next

sleepover this coming Friday.

If all went well, that's when Marion could reveal the big surprise!

By Tuesday, things were falling into place.

Mrs. Ballard had called Amy's mom, Ellie's parents, and Liz's dad. They had all said yes, their daughters could go. And they'd agreed to keep the trip a secret!

Marion was so excited. Being a very organized person, she decided to create a schedule for the weekend. There was *lots* to do up at the cabin. Did her friends know how to ski? Would they want to learn? She needed to know.

In school, Marion walked up to Liz at her locker. It was the end of the day. Kids were packing up to go. "Oh, hey, Liz," said Marion. She tried to sound casual. "Do you know how to ski?"

Liz's eyes lit up. "Cross-country skiing?" she replied. "I've been a few times." Liz closed her locker. "Why?"

"Oh! Um . . . why?" Marion echoed. "No reason. I like skiing too." She didn't know what else to say. So she just stopped talking. And smiled a big smile.

"O-*kay*," Liz replied. She gave Marion a suspicious look.

Ugh, thought Marion. That had *not* gone well.

She had to be much sneakier! Otherwise, she was totally going to mess up this surprise.

Chapter 3

A Snowy Surprise!

Marion did a little better with Ellie and Amy.

Marion asked Amy if she owned any skis. "I'm looking for a pair to borrow," Marion fibbed. She figured a little lie wouldn't hurt, since she was about to tell her friends the truth!

Amy said no. "Sorry. I do have a

pair of snowshoes you could borrow.
I love snowshoeing."

Aha, thought Marion. She'd have
to remember that.

For Ellie, Marion made a quiz.
"It's a How Well Do You Know Your
Friend? quiz," Marion explained.

"You tell me how many questions I got right about you."

Ellie eagerly started reading it. Marion felt very clever.

Ellie zipped through the first two questions. They were about Ellie's favorite color (red, of course) and food (popcorn, correct!).

But Ellie paused at question three.

"Favorite *snow sport*?" Ellie read aloud. "Hmm, weird question. But I guess maybe sledding?"

By the time Friday came, Marion was so relieved. Secrets were hard work. She wanted to tell her friends everything!

That evening, at Marion's house, the girls clearly knew *something* was up.

"What's going on?" Amy asked.

"Why are you so excited?" Ellie added.

"Yeah," said Liz. "And why did you want everyone here before we could come up to your room?"

Marion was leading the way upstairs. "You're about to find out."

She stopped in front of her closed bedroom door.

"SURPRISE!" she cried as she threw the door open.

The girls crowded in the doorway. Marion's bedroom was a winter wonderland!

Dozens of hand-cut paper snow-flakes dangled from the ceiling.

A large white fleece bedspread covered Marion's bed. It looked like a big snowdrift.

And Marion's windows were frosted around the edges with fake snow spray.

While her friends took it all in, Marion shared her big news. "Tomorrow morning," she said, "we are all going to a ski cabin." Marion beamed. "For the whole weekend! There's no school on Monday. So we get to stay two nights!"

The girls stared at Marion in stunned silence.

Then they looked at one another—and started to whoop and cheer!

"But wait!" Liz said. "I have to ask my parents."

"I have to pack!" Ellie said.

"I don't have skis!" Amy said.

Marion sat down on her bed. "No, it's okay!" she explained. "My mom and dad and I took care of all that."

She told them that their parents already knew. They had even packed the girls' coats and extra clothes.

"And don't worry," Marion said. "The cabin has lots of equipment—extra skis, boots, snowshoes. We'll have everything we need!"

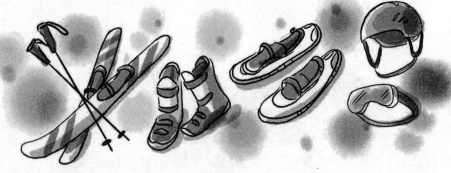

Just then, Marion's cat, Ollie, ran into the room. He jumped onto Marion's bed. Then he curled up in her lap and began to purr.

"Yes, Ollie," Marion said to him. "You're coming too!"

Ellie beamed. "Wow, Marion! You really did think of everything."

"I am so excited!" Amy added.

"Me too," said Liz. "And *now* I get it. This is why you asked if I know how to ski."

Marion burst out laughing. "I'm not good at keeping secrets from you guys!"

Welcome to
the Ski Cabin!

Beep-beep, beep-beep, beep-beep!

Marion's alarm clock went off really early the next morning. But the girls were up and dressed in no time. They were all just so excited to get on the road. Mr. Ballard served pancakes. Mrs. Ballard packed up the minivan. Then all the girls piled in.

"Do we have everyone?" Marion's mom asked from the driver's seat. With Marion, Gabby, plus three friends, all the seats were full.

Ollie let out a *mew*. He was tucked safely in the cat carrier by Marion's feet.

"That's everyone!" Mr. Ballard said in the front passenger seat. "Off we go."

The drive to the cabin was two hours long. But it passed quickly in a blur of fun. Five games of I

Spy. Three rounds of the Alphabet Game. Gabby handed out tins of trail mix halfway through.

The highway climbed into the mountains. The ground became snow covered. The snow got deeper and deeper the higher they went. They took an exit and drove along a twisty country road. Finally, they turned in to a driveway. At the end was a house made of wood and stone. The roof was piled high with snow.

"Welcome to the cabin!" Marion announced when they pulled up. The girls all climbed out of the van.

Marion led her friends inside and gave them a tour. First was a large mudroom. There were lots of pegs for hanging coats, cubbies for hats and mittens, and a place for all the boots.

The living room had comfy couches and a stone fireplace. Marion pointed out the game cabinet. It was packed with board games and decks of cards.

Down a short hall was a bedroom with three sets of bunk beds. "We call it the bunk room," Marion said.

Gabby ran in with her backpack. "I get a top bunk!" she called.

Last, Marion showed them the equipment room. Just as she'd promised, it was filled with skis, poles, boots, sleds, and snowshoes. There were even bins of extra neck warmers and ski socks.

"Want to test some of it out?" Marion asked. "We could start on the easy hiking trail in the backyard."

The girls agreed excitedly. Amy and Ellie decided to try out some snowshoes. Liz and Marion pulled down cross-country skis.

They all got bundled up.

Marion popped into the kitchen
to tell her parents their plan. They
were kneeling on the floor in front
of Ollie's carrier.

"Mom, Dad, we're—" Marion stopped when her parents didn't look up. "What's the matter?"

Mr. Ballard moved a dish of cat food closer to the carrier. "Ollie doesn't want to come out," he explained.

Marion knelt down and peeked in at Ollie. Sure enough, he was curled up way in the back. "Come on, Ollie," Marion sang to him. "Here, sweet boy." She patted her lap, beckoning him.

But Ollie stayed put.

"Let's try to be patient," Marion's mom suggested. "He'll come out when he's hungry." She stood up and helped Marion up too. "You go outside and have fun with your friends."

Mr. Ballard pulled tins of tea and hot cocoa powder out of a shopping bag. "I'll have some of the *best* tea ready when you get back," he said. "And hot cocoa," he added with a wink.

Whose Tracks?

"Wait up!" Liz called to the others. "I'm coming."

She swung her arms, working hard to make it up a hill on the trail. Marion, Ellie, and Amy waited for her at the top.

"Sorry," Liz said, catching her breath. "I stopped to check out the trees back there. I think they're

cedars. There are way more ever-
green trees up here than in Santa
Vista!"

The girls stood there a moment,
taking in the beautiful snowy scen-
ery. The woods were so peaceful.

Marion led them as they continued on the trail. Since it made a loop around her cousin's property, there was no chance of getting lost. And now they weren't far from where the trail would lead back out into the cabin's yard.

Marion looked back at her friends. They were all doing so well! Liz said she felt rusty on skis. But she had only fallen once! And now she was plowing through deep snow, no problem.

Ellie had never gone snowshoeing before. But Amy had shown her how to put the snowshoes on and shared some tips. Now the two of them were trekking side by side. *Crunch, crunch, crunch* through the dry snow.

Amy stopped suddenly. "Look!" she whispered. The girls looked at what she was pointing to.

There, leading into a bramble, were animal tracks.

"What do you think made those?" Marion asked.

Amy pulled her wildlife guide out of her coat pocket. "Let's see," she said. She flipped through pages. "Maybe a rabbit!" Amy said. "See the spacing between the sets of prints? Whatever made them was hopping!"

The girls continued
on. They noticed more
tracks as they went.

"So many footprints!"
said Marion.

The girls moved along
the trail as quietly as they
could. Marion
watched for
motion on
all sides. Every
time snow fell off the
trees, she jumped a little.

They saw many more bunny
tracks. But no bunnies.

"I guess they're pretty good at staying hidden," Marion said, feeling a twinge of disappointment as they returned to the cabin.

Spa Visit

Ollie was still in his carrier. The girls sat in a circle nearby, drinking hot cocoa.

Marion hoped Ollie would be curious enough to come out. But he didn't. Was it possible the car ride had made him feel funny?

Marion decided she would check on him again after their next activity.

Spa time!

"A spa?" Amy said.

"Ooh! Are we getting our nails done?" Ellie asked eagerly.

Marion nodded. "Manicures *and* pedicures!" She knew Ellie would love it. But Amy and Liz didn't look so sure. "There are lots of other relaxing things to do there too. Let's go and I'll show you."

Mrs. Ballard gave the girls a ride in the van. The spa was a few minutes down the country road. A woman at the front desk welcomed them. She handed them a spa menu.

Nail Salon

Whirlpool Tub

Meditation Room

Yoga Studio

"There's a pool?" Amy asked.

The woman nodded. "A mineral pool. Heated to a perfectly relaxing eighty degrees."

"And yoga!" said Liz, looking up from the menu. "I'd love to take a swim and try yoga."

Amy nodded. "Me too."

"Marion thought you might," said Mrs. Ballard. She reached into her bag. "So your parents packed these, too." She handed Amy and Liz their bathing suits and comfy yoga clothes.

Amy and Liz looked at Marion in wonder. "Wow, Marion," Amy said. "I knew you were organized. But—"

"This is impressive," Liz said.

Marion beamed. It made her happy that she knew her friends so well.

The girls split up. Marion and
Ellie went off to the nail salon.
They picked their favorite colors of
polish. Then they soaked their feet
in bubbly tubs.

Amy and Liz got changed. They slid into the mineral pool. Amy did laps. Liz enjoyed floating and listening to the underwater music.

Then they dried off and met the yoga instructor. By the end of their session, they had learned new yoga poses.

The sun was setting as they rode home. Amy and Liz admired Marion and Ellie's fancy nails. Ellie and Marion wanted to hear about the pool.

As soon as they reached the cabin, Marion went straight to Ollie's carrier. "Ollie, we're back," Marion said, looking inside.

The carrier was empty.

"Ollie?" Marion called.

Marion heard a soft *mew* behind her.

She turned around. Ollie was under the kitchen table. Marion knelt down and reached out her hand.

Ollie came over

and let Marion pick him up.

"Oh, Ollie!" Marion cried. She cuddled her cat close. "You're feeling better?"

Marion rushed outside, cradling Ollie in her arms. "Look, everyone! Look who came out—"

Ellie turned toward Marion. She had her finger to her lips. "Shhhh . . ."

Amy pointed at something to Marion's left. Liz and Mrs. Ballard were looking at it too.

Marion turned.

In the front yard were two white bunnies. No! Marion blinked. There were three. Four! Five white bunnies! They were hard to see at first. Their fur blended so well with the snow.

Marion tried to stay absolutely still. She didn't want to scare them away.

The bunnies' ears stood straight up. They sniffed the air, on alert for danger.

In Marion's arms, Ollie twitched. Suddenly he sprang to the ground.

"Ollie!" Marion called. "No!"

Chapter 7

Walking in a Winter Wonderland

In a flash the bunnies scattered. They made five trails of footprints in the snow as they ran for the woods.

"Ollie!" Marion snapped. She quickly scooped him up. She took him back inside. "You scared them away!"

Ollie was wriggling. So Marion

gently put him down. Ollie darted into the kitchen and disappeared into his carrier.

"Oh, Ollie," Marion said softly. "I'm sorry I snapped at you." She sat down in front of the carrier. "Please come back out."

Marion looked at her cat's food dish. It looked like he had eaten some food while they were gone. But not much.

Marion wished she hadn't yelled. She knew Ollie wouldn't hurt the bunnies. He was just curious.

"Ollie?" Marion tried again.

But Ollie looked away and put his head down on his front paws.

Marion sighed. *I guess he wants to be left alone,* she thought. She hoped he would feel better in the morning.

Marion hopped out of her bunk bed. Sunlight streamed in the window. She squinted as she looked outside. Wow! It had snowed overnight. The trees looked like they'd been dipped in icing. And the back deck of the cabin was covered. It looked like a winter wonderland.

"You guys!" she whispered to her friends. Amy, Liz, and Ellie were still sound asleep. Gabby, too. "It snowed! Let's get dressed and go see how deep it is!"

Ellie groaned and rolled over. She pulled her quilt over her head.

Amy sat up and rubbed her eyes.

"What time is it?" Liz asked.

Marion checked. "Seven o'clock," she replied. "Rise and shine!"

It took several tries. Eventually, Marion convinced the girls to get up. They sleepily pulled on long underwear. Then socks. And snow

pants, coats, hats, and mittens. As
they pulled on their boots, the girls'
eyelids were still heavy.

But outside, the frosty
air woke them up.

"Whoa!" cried
Amy. "It must have
snowed a foot!" The
snow on the front step
was up to her knees.

"Look at the van!"
Marion exclaimed. It was a mound
of snow—completely buried.

Liz went over to the van. She
scraped snow off a side window.

She pressed it into a ball. "It's good snow for making a snowman!"

They worked together to roll a big snowball for the bottom. Then Amy and Ellie made the middle ball while Marion and Liz rolled the head.

Ellie stepped back to look at their work. "Hmm," she said. "Let's make it a snow queen." She found a long stick to be the queen's staff. Liz made a crown out of twigs. Amy packed extra snow around the bottom of the snow queen. It looked like she was wearing a long robe. Marion added icicle earrings.

"Nice!" said Mr. Ballard. He and Gabby had come outside with the camera. "Let's get a photo of all of you together."

The girls posed around their snow queen. Mr. Ballard snapped a bunch of photos of them.

"Everybody say 'snowball fight'!" Gabby called.

"Snowball fight?" the girls said together.

A snowball came flying at them.

It hit Marion in the arm.

"Gabby!" Marion shouted with a giggle. "You want a snowball fight? You got it!"

The snow started flying in all directions.

Chapter 8

Snow Worries

The girls came back inside covered in snow. They peeled off their layers. Clumps of snow splatted onto the mudroom floor.

"Brrr!" said Marion. "It's cold out there."

Ellie went to warm up by the fire. "It's *really* cold," she agreed. "You think the bunnies are okay?"

The bunnies! thought Marion. They hadn't seen any sign of them outside. Their prints from last night had been erased by the fresh snow.

"They must be used to the cold," Liz said. "Right? I mean, they do *live* here."

Marion spotted Amy's wildlife guide on the coffee table.

"Amy," Marion said, "does your book say what kind of bunnies they could be?"

Amy flipped through her book. "There is a section in the back. . . ." She found the page she was looking for. "Here! Mammals of the Sierra Nevada Mountains."

Ellie was reading over her shoulder. "There!" Ellie pointed out. "That looks like the bunnies we saw." Ellie looked more closely, then laughed. "But guess what? They're not bunnies!"

Marion frowned. "What?" she said. Liz looked confused too.

Amy turned the book around to show them.

"They're snowshoe hares," Amy
said. She read some info: "'Hares
are a bit larger than rabbits, with
longer hind legs and longer ears.
They have especially large feet that
help them move on top of the snow.
Their brown fur turns snow-white
in the winter.'"

Liz nodded. "So they're definitely fine," she said. "They're actually *built* for the snow."

Marion felt relieved. They didn't have to worry about the bunnies—er, *hares*. They were right at home in the mountains.

Now if only we could say the same for Ollie. Poor Ollie still wasn't feeling well. As Marion sat by the fire, an idea was dawning on her. *Home,* she thought. *Maybe Ollie doesn't feel at home here.*

Marion went into the kitchen to check on her cat. The girls followed. Ollie was still in his carrier. But he was resting closer to the front now.

"Maybe he's not sick at all," Marion said to her friends. "Maybe he's just homesick. He isn't used to the cabin."

"That could be it," Amy agreed.

Ellie spoke up. "Think of all the pets we've watched at The Critter Club," she said. "Sometimes they don't eat as well as they do at home."

"Yeah," said Liz. "Sometimes they're not as playful."

Marion looked at the clock. It was nearly lunchtime. Tomorrow they would be driving home. Marion had planned to pack their last afternoon with activities. Sledding. Ice-skating. Maybe even some downhill skiing.

They were big and exciting plans for her and her friends.

But it didn't feel right.

"Guys," said Marion, "do you mind if we have a quiet afternoon? Here with Ollie?" She reached out and petted his head gently. Ollie let her. "I think he could use the company."

Amy smiled and nodded.

"Of course," said Liz.

"That sounds like a good plan," added Ellie.

Chapter 9

Taking Care of Ollie

The girls had a quiet, cozy afternoon in the cabin. Marion gently moved Ollie's carrier into the living room so he could enjoy the fire too. The girls sat around the coffee table. They did a big jigsaw puzzle. Then they played cards.

Through it all, the girls took turns sitting by Ollie. They showered him

with attention. They spoke to him
softly and petted his head and front
paws.

The sun was getting low outside.
Marion was next to Ollie's carrier.
She tried patting her lap, inviting
Ollie to come out.

Marion was surprised as Ollie
stood up. He stepped out and
rubbed his head against Marion's
knee. Then he climbed into her lap
and sat down.

No one said a word. Ellie did a silent happy dance. Amy smiled a huge smile. Liz gave Marion a thumbs-up.

A little while later, Ollie got up. He slinked slowly around the coffee table. He stopped to say hello to each of the girls with a soft *mew*.

"*Now* he's starting to seem like his old self," Marion said.

The true test was at dinnertime.

Mr. Ballard put out dinner for everyone. The kids sat down at the table. Meanwhile, Mrs. Ballard filled Ollie's dish with fresh food. Then she and Mr. Ballard sat down too.

Ollie sat in the kitchen doorway. He looked at them. He looked at his food dish. He looked at them again.

Then he scampered over to the dish. He buried his face in his cat food.

"Yay!" Marion and the girls cheered.

Chapter 10

Home Is Where
the Heart Is

The next morning, the girls helped
pack up the van. Then they all
climbed inside.

"Do we have everyone?" Mrs.
Ballard asked. "Let's make sure we
have as many as we came with."

Marion laughed. They usually
only did that on class field trips.
She knew she got her planning and

organization skills from her mom!

Just then, Mr. Ballard pointed out the front windshield. "Girls! Look!"

Five snowshoe hares were scampering across the snowy driveway.

The leader stopped. The others did too. The hares turned and stared at the van.

Then they hurried on. They hopped up and over a snowdrift.

The girls watched as they disappeared into the backyard.

"Aww," said Amy. "It's like they came to say good-bye."

"Good-bye, snowshoe hares!" Ellie called as the van pulled out of the driveway.

"Good-bye, cabin!" Liz added.

Marion laughed. "See you again soon!"

Back in Santa Vista, the van made stops at each of the girls' houses. Finally, the Ballards pulled into their own driveway.

Marion took Ollie's carrier inside. She put it down and opened the door.

Ollie scampered right out. He jumped up on the sofa by the sunny window. He curled up on the arm— his favorite spot.

Minutes later, Ollie was taking a cat nap.

Marion flopped onto the sofa. It was bittersweet to be home. She was happy she and her friends had had such a fun weekend— and that Ollie was feeling better. But she was sad it was over.

Then her face lit up when she saw the family photo album on the side table.

The photo Dad took!
She was going to need a copy.

the CRITTER club

Join the club!

31901065228738

Visit CritterClubBooks.com for activities, excerpts, and the series trailer!